TEMPTRESS

Fallon Raynes

Acknowledgements

Thank you, Janet, for keeping me on the right path. Your insights are greatly appreciated. I'm happy you are in my life!

Thank you, Savannah at Ignitiveify for this awesome cover! Your creativity never ceases to amaze me!

To Bob, thank you for always fitting me into your schedule. I'm glad I was sent your way!

To my Family and friends, your kind words after reading my stories keeps me writing. I love you ALL! THANK YOU!

To Craig Martelle for the awesome opportunity to be included in a great project! It was a welcome and appreciate experience that I was excited and still shocked to be included in.

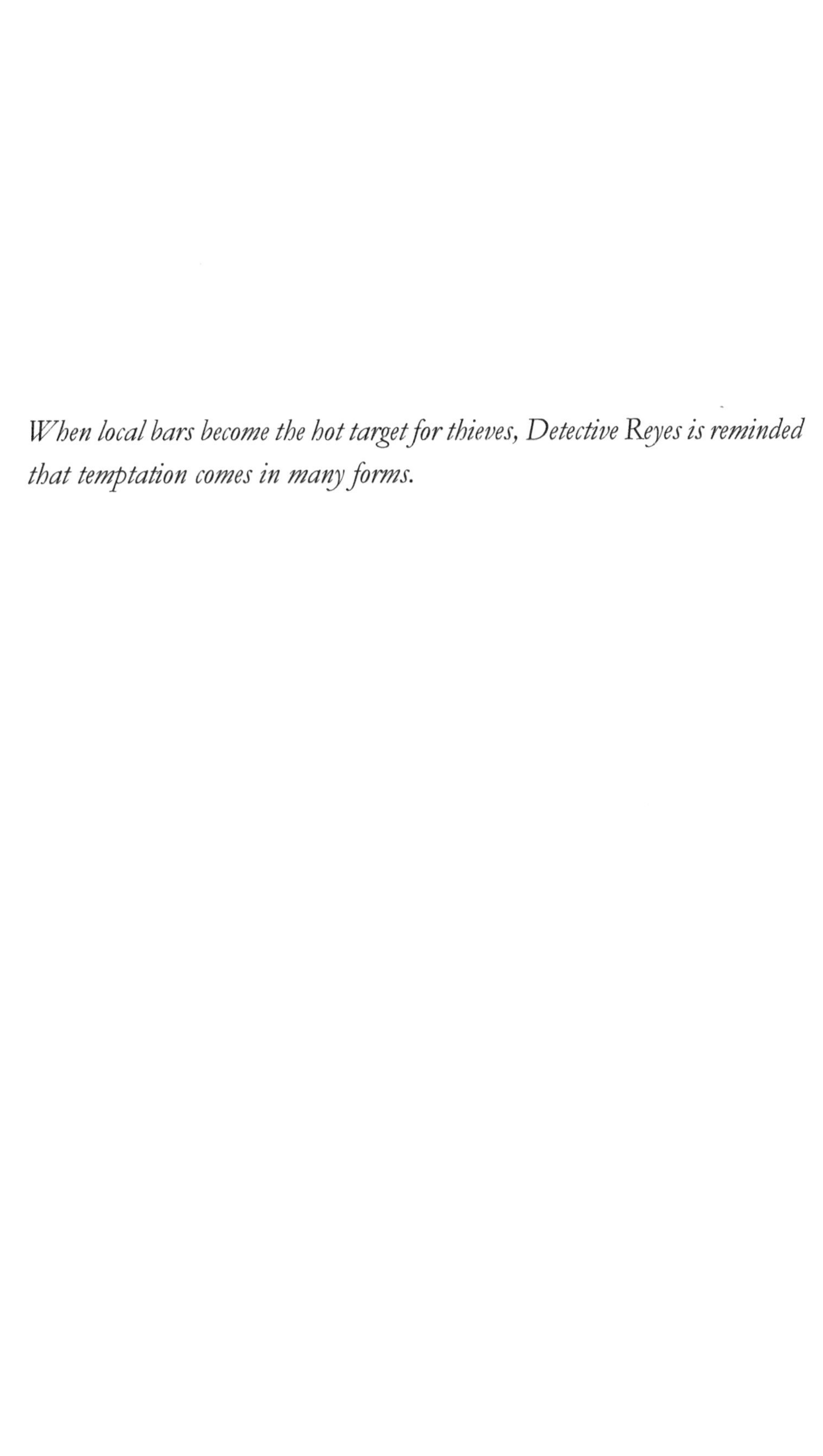

When local bars become the hot target for thieves, Detective Reyes is reminded that temptation comes in many forms.

Chapter 1

A vision in a red dress and spiky, black heels fluttered into the bar. Her short, flared skirt danced at her long legs from the rush of the evening breeze coming through the open door. She brushed a strand of flame-red hair behind her ear. The door closed, darkening the room. The lady in red stood there at the entrance as she searched the dimly lit surroundings. Behind the bar was Frank, the owner of the outdated bar called Lucky's. He stood frozen with his gaze on the woman, his mouth agape.

Grady smirked, thinking the guy's sad old eyes had probably never seen the likes of this gal. His gal, in fact, and aptly nicknamed "Red," her favorite color.

Finally, she found what she was searching for—or more accurately, *whom*. Grady grinned and made a "tipping of the hat" motion. Red's full lips turned up in a smile as she sashayed over to him. He held out his arms, and she threw herself into his embrace. Her skirt twirled up as he swung her around a few times before setting her down for a kiss. He sucked in a deep breath of air and tasted her sweet perfume. He looked around, noticing the patrons at the bar and pool table were just as enthralled with them as he had hoped they would be.

She pulled herself away and blushed demurely. *Ah, she's good,* Grady thought. He steadied her and offered the chair next to the pool table. The sharp smacking of the balls resumed. He smirked, winked, and then headed to the bar to get her a drink and refill his whiskey.

When he returned, he gave her another quick wink as he set an icy mug of beer in front of her. She took a quick sip and seductively licked the foam off her lips. He had to admit, Red was hard to ignore. And that was exactly what they wanted.

Her grand entrance had actually worked. No one had seen Kent come in and slip to the back office. Their plan was in motion. When her knees started to bounce slightly—a hint that she was getting anxious—Grady pushed down on them gently. He took his thumb and started tracing circles on the fair skin of her inner thigh.

He nodded slightly toward the bar, and she casually turned to look in that direction. The bartender's eyes locked with hers, and she ran her tongue along her top lip while Grady's hand wandered up her skirt. She was definitely the main attraction this evening. Grady continued the play, stroking the inside of her leg with his rough hand. His phone buzzed in his pocket—once, then two more times.

That was the signal. *Show time.* Grady slid Red's chair closer to him, put his arm around her back, hand on her shoulder. He lightly squeezed three times to relay the message. Red stiffened, and he looked directly into those green eyes and gave her a smile of assurance. *Everything will be fine.*

She picked up her mug and sucked in a small amount of the foam. Looking over the rim of the glass, she batted her lashes at Frank. She slowly lowered the mug. Gave a provocative smile, one eyebrow raised. She had all the moves.

Grady glared at the bartender and stood up, knocking his chair to the floor. He hollered at Frank, "Get your eyes off my lady!"

Red grabbed for Grady's arm and pleaded for him to sit down. Grady pulled his arm out of her hold, and stalked over to Frank. Leaning across the bar top, sticking his finger in the bartender's face, he said through gritted teeth, "You've been ogling her since she walked in. Keep your eyes to yourself, old man!"

Frank had backed up against the liquor bottles, which clanked and teetered dangerously. Somehow, none fell to the floor. Fear was etched across his face. He threw his hands up and said, "Don't want no trouble, man. I don't want your girl."

One of the two patrons sitting at the bar hopped out of the way, taking his drink with him. The other man sat there and slurred, "Don't both-errr F-Frank, man."

Grady whipped around to stab his finger into the drunk's chest. "Shut it," Grady growled.

The guy swayed and fell off his stool to the dusty floor. His buddy tried to pick him up but promptly fell over when his legs gave out—clearly inebriated as well. Grady wanted to laugh at their mayhem but refrained, turning his gaze back on Frank, who had moved farther down the bar.

Two pool players headed in their direction, pool sticks in hand, ready to intervene. Red threw her hands out to stop them. The tall, skinny one grabbed her by the arm and shoved her out of the way, causing a yelp to escape her lips. Upon hearing this, Grady spun around just in time to see Red lose her balance and fall to the floor.

He lost his cool, face reddening, eyes narrowing, throwing a barstool out of his way as he stalked over to the guy, whose emaciated body could barely hold up his filthy jeans. Grady's fist connected nicely with the man's ugly face.

Grady had been counting on just this sort of scuffle to keep the attention on them—at least for now. He also thoroughly enjoyed this part of the con.

***

Kent was holed up just out of sight in the dark hallway. He heard Red's yelp. He sneaked a peek around the corner and saw Grady land a fist into the gangly dude's face. All eyes were on the chaos, and that was his cue. He left out the side door he had used just moments earlier. Grady and Red would be coming out shortly, and he would be waiting with the car running at the front door.

Kent was quick with small, old safes. He had been cracking those since his alcoholic, abusive father had taught him, way back when.

The front door of the bar slammed opened, interrupting his trip down memory lane. Grady had a smile on his face, and Red was flushed as they raced to the car. Kent was driving off before the doors were closed.

"How much did the old geezer have?" Grady asked as they headed toward the expressway.

"About six grand, give or take." Kent checked the rearview mirror to glance at Red. "How are you doin', girl?"

"I'm okay. That skinny bastard didn't have much in him, but I made it look good." She smirked at Kent in the mirror, who chortled at her reply.

He then turned to look at Grady in the passenger seat. "How'd you do, buddy?" When Grady turned to face him, a scowl on his lips, Kent jerked his head back as he saw the shiner for the first time. He winced at the sight. "Damn."

Grady gently touched his eye. "Yeah, I was doin' just fine till the one guy knocked me from behind. Cheap shot. But the black eye didn't come from him—I hit the corner of the table. Asshole. But I laid him out. All's well that ends well, and all that crap," he said with a Cheshire-cat grin.

Kent chuckled. "Sounds like you had fun."

Grady said, "Yeah, just get us to the motel in one piece, will ya?"

Chapter 2

Detective Reyes answered the phone at his desk early at the Midland Law Enforcement Center Wednesday morning. He listened, grunted a few times as a response, then wrote down the information he was given. Hanging up the phone without saying goodbye, he eyeballed his partner, who sat at a desk across from him.

Detective Hannah merely stared at him, waited. They'd known each other a long time, and sometimes words were not necessary.

Finally, Reyes spoke. "A break-in over at Lucky's—ya know, Frank's place. Someone stole money out of his safe."

"Something you can handle alone?" Hannah motioned to the paperwork on his desk. "I can certainly keep busy here."

Reyes nodded, "Yeah, I've got this covered. Sounds like I'm getting the better deal anyway. I'll leave you to it." He smiled wide as he grabbed his coffee and headed for the door.

He hit every single red light while heading to Lucky's. What normally should have taken ten minutes was doubled. That pissed him off—traffic.

Everyone knew Frank at Lucky's, but the man served fewer and fewer patrons over the years. Since craft beer had become more sought after in Michigan, bars like this were feeling the hit. Frank was hanging in there, though. Sometimes even the younger crowd showed up and raised some hell at the old bar. Reyes knew that always made Frank's cash register a little fuller. But mostly the bar catered to the regulars during the week. So this robbery surprised Reyes, as this was not a hot place for money, to put it mildly. And that made him curious. Very curious, indeed. The thief wasn't looking for a lot of money, it appeared. Small-time crook. Or maybe he had been disappointed in the haul from Lucky's. Still, it was strange.

Reyes slipped his gloves on, walked in, and saw Frank sitting at the bar. He looked broken. The detective spoke in a soft voice, "Hey, Frank. Sorry to meet under these conditions."

Frank turned. "Hey, Ricky. Me too. Me too." He saw the gloves on the detective's hands, and his shoulders sunk a little more.

Reyes caught the change. "So, tell me what happened, as much as you know."

Frank took in a deep breath, let it out. "I came in this morning, counted the till. When I went to put the money in the safe, the damn thing was empty. Open and empty." He dropped his head into his hands. "It's all gone, Ricky. Gone! I don't understand. Everything was locked when I came in."

"Can you show me around?" Reyes said. "I'd like to take a look at everything."

Frank looked up and nodded, slid off the stool. "Follow me."

Reyes eyeballed the surroundings as the men headed toward the office. He'd already noted that the front door did not appear to have been tampered with. The long, skinny, horizontal windows at the top of the bar were the typical style that didn't open. Each was still intact. Reyes stopped beside the alley door and noted the wood frame was untouched. He pulled the door open with gloved hands and examined the lock. Nothing looked like it had been jimmied. He followed Frank into the office and saw the open safe behind the old wooden desk.

Kneeling down Reyes saw no signs of forced entry on the safe, which had an old-style combination lock. Nothing fancy.

Reyes straightened with his eyes on the solitary window in the office—also one that did not open. The frame was untouched. He walked around the office looking for anything the thief may have left behind, but nothing caught his attention. He hadn't really expected that, but hey… a guy can dream.

"Frank, did you find anything else missing?"

"No, my gun goes upstairs with me at night, and as I mentioned, the money was still in the till. I didn't put it away last night. I was a bit frazzled after the fight."

Reyes's ears perked up. "Fight? You didn't mention that. Did you call it in?"

"Yeah, your guys showed up and took my complaint. The troublemaker had left with a drop-dead gorgeous redhead by the time they got here." Frank paused, chewed on his lip. "You know, that dame was part of the problem, actually."

"Yeah? How so?" Reyes's interest was piqued.

Frank ran through the events that had taken place the night before, starting with when the lady had entered the establishment. Reyes jotted it down in his notepad, all the while forming a mini movie of the evening his mind. With the lack of evidence for a straight-up break-in, he put his attention on this bar fight. It might have been a diversion. The thief could have stolen the money while the fight was taking place.

It was the oldest trick in the book. Magicians used it. And so did con men. While every eye was focused on the diversion, no one ever noticed the quarter disappear, so to speak. Maybe, just maybe, he had his first clue.

He questioned Frank some more about the patrons and how well he knew them. The only newbies were the man and woman. Reyes was really liking this couple for the ruse. He looked around the bar and asked, "Did you ever install any cameras in here?"

"No. I don't know anything about them, and I wouldn't know what to do with them anyway. You know I don't use that new technology."

Reyes nodded, knowing Frank didn't even have a cell phone. The bar owner was a simple man.

The detective excused himself, went out to his car, and grabbed the fingerprinting kit he kept in his glove box. Then he went to work dusting for prints.

The old safe was dimpled and wouldn't pull any clean prints, but he did it anyway. For Frank's benefit, mostly. To reassure the old guy that everything was being done to uncover the robber, or robbers.

Reyes then dusted doorknobs, door frames, and any surface he thought the thief may have laid his hands on. He snapped photos and, last, took Frank's prints.

"Thanks, Ricky. I appreciate you doing this." Frank's brows furrowed at the dusty mess all over the office. "Can I clean up now that you're done? Or does this need to look like a crime scene for a while?"

"Nah, go ahead and clean, get things in order, Frank, I have everything I need. Sorry to make such a mess, but maybe we'll find something helpful." Reyes gave a tight-lipped smile, trying to convey encouragement he didn't feel. Frank was of the generation where you helped people in need. To see him get taken like this was heartbreaking. He knew Frank didn't have a lot to survive on. Reyes vowed to do his damndest to get that money back for his old friend.

They said their goodbyes, and Reyes stepped outside. He looked around the parking lot, at the building itself, and then at the surrounding buildings. No visible surveillance cameras anywhere.

Frank had mentioned that when he and his customers were interviewed by the cops last night, no one had seen the vehicle the couple had left in. Reyes had been hoping for a video to shed some light on the getaway car. He hopped in his truck and drove around the area, looking for security cameras. Or any other inspiration.

Chapter 3

Thursday Morning

Detective Reyes was in the LEC the next morning looking over the reports that had come through for the fingerprints. Most of the prints were smudged, and the only clean set of prints matched Frank's. He'd had no luck with security cameras, either. Frank had given him a detailed description of the couple who had been at the bar that night. Reyes had a strong feeling they were in on the heist. But where to start when there were no leads?

Yet.

He raked his hand through his brown hair, determined to find focus and get justice for Frank.

"You look like you could use this." Hannah set a cup of coffee down in front of Reyes as he passed his desk.

"I've already had three, but thanks." Reyes picked up the cup.

"Any leads from those prints?"

"No. Frank's were the only match. The rest were unusable. I'm going to hazard a guess and say the thief was wearing gloves. The safe didn't pull up much. It was an old safe, lots of dimples. No cameras in the area to pinpoint a getaway vehicle. Our only chance is they hit again—and screw up." Reyes frowned, setting his cup down. "At least that's how it seems right now."

"Well, Frank has always been good with faces, so maybe that will help."

"Yes, the details he gave were perfect."

Hannah nodded and looked down at his desk. He picked up the piece of paper lying next to his phone. It was new lead for a case that had come in while Reyes was out yesterday. "Well, perhaps this will interest you." He tossed the paper over to his partner's desk. "There was a stolen car called in yesterday. A connection with the robbery?" He shrugged. "Maybe, huh? They found the car near the edge of town. Let's go check it out."

"Let's," Reyes said without hesitation. He'd take any lead he could get.

Chapter 4

Kent and Grady had each taken a few hundred for themselves the minute they'd arrived at the motel. The rest they stashed in a vent in their motel room. Red was out on a food run. When she returned, they would discuss their next steps over a few hamburgers. They wanted to make two more hits, if they could. Then they'd lie low for a while. The two old friends had grown up in the Tri-Cities. Bay City, Midland, and Saginaw were easy to access from their cheap hideout near the US-10 exit.

Red was the newest to the team. She was a hot looker who had been seeing a guy Grady had worked a job with before. She had run into Grady the night she and the guy broke up. Cried on Grady's shoulder, she did. And that was that. She was "in." Kent suspected she'd get bored with him soon enough, though. Red came across like she was destined for more than hanging around two common thieves. She wore nice things. Expensive things. Things Grady couldn't afford; he liked to fight and couldn't hold down a job.

A car door slammed shut, and Grady went to the window, pulled the curtain aside, and peeked out. It was Red, juggling some McDonald's bags and a drink tray.

Grady opened the door with a love-sick grin on his face. Red glided in wearing red shorts and matching tank top and kissed his cheek. "Food's up, guys," she said as she dropped the fast food on the small table. The smell had Kent's stomach growling, and he realized it had been a long time since he'd last eaten. He shoved some fries in his mouth just as Red was heading back out the door. "Be right back," she said with a wave of her finger. Upon returning, she carried a few other shopping bags. Red sure was on fire to spend the dough.

The group settled in around the little table with Red on Grady's lap—there were only two chairs in the room. Grady was feeding Red fries as she giggled. Kent just shook his head. The two were nuts for each other; that much was clear. The display they made last night had been part of the plan, but he knew Grady was falling hard for this little minx. He hoped she didn't break his heart. Grady was like the brother Kent never had.

The trio finished their feast and cleared the table. Kent grabbed the drawings of the two locations they could possibly rob tonight. Ray's Tavern in particular was preferred. If the parking lot wasn't too busy, they would hit there first. Kent and Grady had already been to all the area bars quite a few times over the past few weeks. They'd gone in separately so as not to draw suspicion. It made a job easier when they'd familiarized themselves with the layout of the establishments and the movements of the staff.

Grady had not been able to get into the office at Jackson's Watering Hole; the door had been locked. And he was almost caught trying to pick the lock. So Ray's was better to try tonight. It had a safe in the office closet that was a combination lock—Kent was a wiz at those. They knew it would be a quick in-and-out. In fact, the bar was similar to Lucky's.

Grady nodded at Kent. "Easy peasy."

"Should be," Kent agreed, rubbing his chin.

They had been left alone to work out these plans, as Red had run off to the bathroom with her bags. She seemed to care less about preparation and more about the spending of the loot. But she was good at her game, and they were happy to oblige her nonchalance.

"What do you boys think?" she said, exiting the bathroom.

Grady gave a low wolf whistle in appreciation.

Kent beamed from ear to ear. "Sexy mama!"

In a blond wig that came down just past her shoulders, Red twirled around in a white, flouncy skirt with red polka dots on it. The red peasant blouse was pulled down low on her shoulders—she was braless, to boot. Red always picked out the flared skirts so they would fly up when Grady twirled her, giving the voyeurs a quick peek at her panties. She was a temptress with a capital T.

"What time are we leaving?" Red asked as she sauntered over to the table. Just as Kent started to respond, she said, "Ooo," and gently caressed the shiner on Grady's face. "We need to cover that up first." She grabbed her bag and pulled out her makeup case. After choosing a tube of skin-colored goo, she applied it around Grady's eye. When she stepped back to admire her work, Kent was surprised to see the black eye was no longer visible. *Impressive. Girl's got skills,* Kent thought.

Grady said, "Feels funny," and raised his hand to touch the area.

Red quickly smacked his hand away. "No touchy. You'll mess it up."

Kent laughed at Grady's expense. "Okay, ten minutes till we head out. Are you guys ready?" He established eye contact with each of them as they simultaneously responded with, "Yep."

Kent rubbed his hands together, then stood. He was more than ready to test their lucky streak, especially with the next bar being such a sure thing. "Okay, then. Gather your stuff, and let's make some scratch."

Chapter 5

Thursday Evening

Grady held Red's hand as he led her into Ray's Tavern with its low lights and loud music rushing from the jukebox. The place had a dance floor with room for a band and a few pool tables. Muffled conversation filled the air while they made their way to the tables near the dance floor. There was one waitress working, and the bartender was behind the bar. The waitress was new, at least to Grady. He hadn't noticed her before; it had only been the bartender whenever he'd scouted the joint. This could be tricky.

Grady glanced around the room as they grabbed a seat. There were a few couples stretched across the bar, keeping to themselves. Not many at the tables. One man sitting at the end of the bar was talking to the bartender. A couple of single guys were standing around the pool table at the back of the room. One of them was racking the balls for the next game. It was a small, quiet crowd. Grady hoped it stayed that way.

"What'll it be, folks?" the petite, dark-haired waitress asked.

"We'll have a couple of drafts, please." Grady smiled, handing her a ten.

She plucked the bill from his fingers. "Comin' right up."

Grady made his way over to the jukebox and saw that there was no song scheduled to play next. He dropped a bunch of quarters in and loaded some tunes to set the mood. They had a few more minutes before it would be dark enough in the alley. Then Kent could slip in the side door from the dark alley without anyone noticing. The fourth song Grady selected was with purpose. He wanted to grab the attention of everyone in the room when it started playing. He and Red had practiced earlier that day behind the motel room. She was a quick study. All eyes would be on them in no time.

The barmaid was dropping off their drinks when he sauntered back to their table. He gave her a quick cowboy nod and took his seat at the table, next to Red. They both took long draws of their drafts. Red had already caught the eye of one of the pool players. She licked the froth off her lips as the guy watched. Grady held in a chuckle. The girl was something else. He couldn't wait to start the show.

Grady and Red flirted with each other while they waited for their cue. The second song came on, and the barmaid headed to the back. Grady watched for her to return while keeping up his end of the flirting. When the third song started to play, Grady could feel the knots forming in his stomach. Red's knee started to bounce—her nervous twitch, so to speak. He slid his hand onto her thigh to gently reassure her, like he had the other night at Lucky's. The waitress still had not returned from the back.

Red raised an eyebrow at Grady, who shrugged. Maybe this wasn't going to work out after all. About the time he had decided to go ahead and text Kent the Code Red signal—effectively nixing the operation—the waitress walked back into view, drying her hands on her apron. Grady and Red visibly relaxed, taking long swigs of their beers. Grady looked around and verified that everyone else was still accounted for. The song stopped. The fourth song came on, and Grady stood up. This song was long, flirty, and contagious. He grinned from ear to ear as he reached for Red's hand, all gentleman-like. "Would you care to dance, ma'am?"

"Why, yes, I would love to, kind sir." Red blushed and giggled as she placed her hand in his like a princess.

Grady sent Red spinning onto the dance floor. She squealed as she twirled, her skirt flying up and out. Her red panties made their debut, and gauging by the crowd's full attention, the peepshow was a hit.

Red took her stance as Grady had taught her. He danced toward her, a routine he knew well. The chicks loved it, and, man, he loved the chicks. Especially this one. Red was his "Baby," and he was excited to play the part of Johnny tonight.

The people started cheering them on as they played out the scene from *Dirty Dancing*. The famous part was coming up. Grady felt the tension from the onlookers as they anticipated it.

Red took off and floated through the air. He caught her. Perfection.

Cheers and whistles erupted from the crowd as he brought her back down and kissed her hard on the lips. Red couldn't wipe the smile off her face as the song ended and the next track Grady had queued started to play.

Everyone went back to what they were doing. Grady's phone buzzed the signal from Kent. It was done. They only had to finish their beers and leave. Grady dropped a five on the table for a tip, then gave Red a passionate kiss, indicating to anyone who was watching that they were ready to leave the bar and light up another room—like a bedroom.

They stood. She wrapped one arm around his middle and didn't take her eyes off his face as he escorted her from the bar.

He couldn't tell if she was still acting or if she was falling for him.

Chapter 6

Kent waited at the curb a few spaces down from the front of the bar, trying to control his accelerated heart rate. *What a rush!* He loved the thrill. He'd sent the code message off to Grady while the car idled, and upon seeing his partners exiting the bar, he let loose a long sigh of relief. It was now 10:30 p.m. and he didn't think they would have enough time to hit the second bar on their list. Besides, that one was a little iffy anyway, as Grady had never been able to put his eyes on the office. The team had figured out these bars picked up on Thursday nights around this area.

Grady let Red slide in the front seat between him and Kent. She was glowing. The bar was pretty soundproof, but Kent could hear the music at the door. When the fourth song had started, he had let a few seconds pass and then entered. He caught part of their act as he casually made his way to the back. The office was unlocked. He was quick and efficient. He saw Red take flight. A heart-stopping sight.

Grady looked around Red at Kent. "I wish you could have seen us. We knocked it out of the park! Red, you were sensational." Grady squeezed her shoulder as he put his arm around her.

"Oh my God! I can't sit still. I want to go back and do it again!" Red bounced in her seat with delight. "That was so much fun!"

"Well, some night when we're all caught up, you'll have to do a repeat for me." Kent laughed as he pulled onto the street, heading to the expressway. With both of them worked up, he knew for sure there was no way they could pull off another heist tonight. "We're headed to our motel home, kids. That's enough for tonight."

"Sounds good to me," Grady murmured as he pulled Red into his chest. She planted a big, wet kiss on his lips.

Here we go with these two, Kent thought with a small grin. *But a damn good team.* In no time, they were on the expressway. They'd be back to the motel and counting their haul in ten minutes.

"When you wanna hit Jackson's?" Grady asked after coming up for air.

Ken said, "Let's see how things go. Maybe tomorrow, hit it at eight-ish before it gets busy. This time, remember, we'll all go in together."

"Tomorrow is Friday. You think it's safe to do? Maybe we should hold off until next week when the place won't be too busy," Red suggested.

"I think it'll be fine." Kent shook it off with a smile at Red, then looked back at the road.

'Yeah, Baby, we've got it covered," Grady said, using her nickname from the routine they had completed.

Still grinning, Kent glanced at the two of them. "Yeah, *Baby.*"

Red shrugged and let it go, but Kent noticed that her smile had faded as she looked out the windshield. Kent turned his focus back to the road.

The trio went silent the rest of the way to the motel. The parking lot held a few more cars in it since they had left. Kent pulled the bag from the trunk. They all went inside. He dropped the bag onto the table and pulled on the zipper. The money was askew in the bottom of the bag; a few of the rubber bands had broken.

Red kept walking to the bathroom and shut the door. Kent looked at Grady and whispered, "You think she's good?"

"Yeah, yeah. I'm sure the high wore off on the way back." Grady glanced back at the bathroom door as if to reassure himself she wasn't listening.

"Because if not, we can take tomorrow on by ourselves. We've done it before." Kent kept his voice low.

"Nah, dude, she's good." Grady nodded his head at the bag. "Let's get this counted so we can relax the rest of the night." They both reached in and grabbed handfuls of money until the bag was empty.

Chapter 7

Reyes drove by the Backdoor Bar on his way home. It was similar to Frank's. He decided to stop in and see what Chief was up to. Maybe do a little scouting to see if he had cameras, in case his place was next. The stolen car had been a bust. There were witnesses that saw a couple of teenagers crash the car and run. He pulled into the alley, parked, and turned off the engine.

He immediately noticed the side door of the bar wasn't lit up like it normally was. He got out of his unmarked car and flipped his cell phone's flashlight on. Looking around, he didn't see anything out of the ordinary.

He continued into the bar and saw a handful of people gathered at the pool tables and a few patrons talking to Chief at the bar. There was a couple necking in the back corner booth. Everything seemed normal, and not too many heads turned to look his way when he entered.

Chief looked up and waved him over. The detective smiled at his tall, burly friend as he made his way over.

"Hey, Chief. How goes it?" He nodded when Chief held up the whiskey bottle with Reyes's favorite label on it. "That sounds good tonight."

Chief poured the whiskey, neat, and brought it over to him. The customers he'd been talking to wandered over to a table near the jukebox. Reyes had Chief to himself for a few minutes. "Pretty quiet tonight for a Thursday, isn't it?"

"Yes and no. It's been pretty steady lately. Tomorrow night, it will be a bigger crowd." The big guy smiled. "How have you been? I haven't seen you in a few weeks. Wife keeping you busy, or is it the mistress?" He winked at the detective.

"The mistress, for sure." Reyes chuckled at Chief's label for his job that keeps him away from his family. "There's a case I'm working on. Mostly the reason I made time to stop in tonight."

"Oh? Why would that involve me? There haven't been any fights in here since last summer."

"I know. There's a case I'm working, like I said. I think they're hitting places like yours. Oh, that reminds me… Did you know your bulb is burnt out in the alley?"

"Weird. I just replaced that thing the other night." Chief scratched his head. "You mind watching the bar while I go grab another bulb and put it in?"

Reyes sipped on his whiskey and nodded. "Go for it."

"Thanks. When I get back, I want to hear more about this case of yours."

Reyes surveyed the room, looking for little red blinking lights to indicate a camera was in use. He didn't see any, or at least they weren't visible to him. He finished his whiskey just as Chief returned wearing a puzzled look on his face and carrying a package of light bulbs.

"That bulb wasn't burnt out. It was loose. Almost loose enough to fall out on someone." Chief rubbed the back of his neck, "I know darn well that I tightened that bulb when I replaced it. And it worked."

"Do you have video cameras? I was glancing around, and I'm not seeing any."

"Not in the alley. I have a few hidden cameras in here and my office. The kind that fit into small spaces. The footage gets loaded to the cloud. My daughter Lucy put them in for me last year after the last fight at the bar."

"Good. Do you think you could get a few put up on the outside tomorrow?"

"Yeah, I'm sure she can do that. Question is, why?"

"Like I mentioned earlier, a few bars like yours are getting hit. Play it safe."

Chief shrugged. "I hear ya. Will do."

Reyes pulled his wallet out and flipped Chief a ten spot. "About that light bulb… I think you might want to check your cloud footage."

"Doubt I'll see anything. I looked at the lock. It wasn't jimmied, and nothing has been touched in here."

"Yeah, maybe they didn't make it inside this time, but that bulb didn't loosen itself, Chief. Call me if you find anything." He pulled his card out and handed it to the bar owner, who agreed to do just that.

Reyes flipped him a wave as he left the bar. If he were a betting man, he'd put money on that call tomorrow. And Reyes *was* a betting man. He slowly pulled out of the alley and made his way around the block, looking for more cameras set up on the few businesses in this area of town.

For whatever reason, he felt it in his gut: the Backdoor Bar was on the hit list. He decided to swing back around to watch the bar for another hour before he went home.

Chapter 8

Friday Morning

Reyes arrived early at the office the next morning. His impromptu stakeout had been unsuccessful. But when he found a message waiting on his desk, he cursed out loud. The thugs had hit again. He was pissed. Ray at Ray's Tavern had noticed his safe was empty at the end of the night. Ray had called the station a little after two that morning. Another detective had taken the call. It appeared he had already done the legwork for him.

The copy of the report was with the message. Reyes sat down at his desk and finished reviewing it. He logged into his computer and brought up the local dive bars on the map. Ray's Tavern was on the other side of town. He grabbed his coffee and headed out, planning to scout the area for video footage. The other detective had mentioned there were no cameras in the establishment. More work to be done. Most likely the prints would be nonexistent, like with Frank's place.

There were only two more bars in town that fit the description. Places that were easier to hit—no visible cameras. He needed to get to Jackson's Watering Hole when it opened at noon. He would grab some lunch, give them a heads-up. He would set up surveillance at Jackson's tonight. He knew time was running out before the thieves moved on to another town. Or worse, someone got hurt trying to be a hero. So far, no one had caught them in the act. And no weapons had yet to be involved. He didn't even want to think about the list of things that could go wrong. Either way, he wanted vindication, and most importantly, to return the money stolen from Frank—a true friend; in fact, more like a father to him than he'd ever had.

He could not fail.

Chapter 9

Reyes's phone buzzed on his way back from Jackson's Watering Hole, and he punched up the call. "Reyes here."

"It's Chief. Can you stop by?" The bar owner sounded antsy, speaking at a fast clip.

"I'm not far from you now. I'll be there in five."

He made it there in four minutes and rushed through the door, anxious to hear what Chief had discovered.

"Thanks for coming so quickly." Chief and his daughter Lucy were standing at the door when Reyes walked in.

"No problem. You seem stressed. What did you find?"

"Lucy has the camera footage on my computer."

As they walked to the tall bar top, Lucy filled him in on setting up the other security cameras outside. Reyes said a small prayer of thanks for the woman's skills.

She motioned for Reyes to have a seat. "Check it out. This is what we saw when I brought up the footage from last week." She clicked to play the video. "As you can see, this is the camera for the back office here. I also have more footage of this guy from other cameras. I saved it all on this thumb drive for you." She dropped the drive into his open palm.

Reyes watched as the video depicted the office door opening. The intruder searched the room and then, *bingo*, a camera shot of this fool's face, up close and personal, as he eyeballed the safe.

"Thanks, Lucy. This is great!"

"There's more footage on that thumb drive, shows him on the other cameras and his other visits here." She slid a piece of paper to Reyes. "Here is a printed picture of his face. It's the best one I could find from all his visits."

Reyes was beyond impressed. "Lucy, this will help me break this case, I can just feel it."

Chief beamed and put his arm around his daughter's shoulders.

Reyes held the thumb drive up, then pocketed it. "Thank you both. This is a hot lead. I need to get back and get this sorted. Do not go near this guy and his accomplices if they come in here. Let us do our job. We'll be here tonight, watching." Reyes gave Chief a stern look.

Chief threw up his hands. "No problem. We'll stay out of the way."

"Thank you." He could barely contain his enthusiasm as he headed back to his car.

Chapter 10

Grady, Kent, and Red walked into the latest soon-to-be victim's bar, where a jukebox was playing a slow song and two couples were glued together on the dance floor. The trio had a different plan to play out tonight. They were here to get in and out quickly, so they could pillage one other place too. Tomorrow, they'd move on.

Red looked at Kent with her pouty lips and held her hand out for some quarters. He dipped into his pocket and handed her a wad. The waitress dropped by the table after Red got up to select her songs. They ordered drafts for themselves and one for Red. She came back and sat down. She leaned into Kent's ear and whispered something. Kent smiled. Grady pulled Red into his lap. He held his arm around her possessively, glaring at Kent.

The barmaid brought the beers back to the table. Kent flipped her some cash to cover the drinks and a tip. They wouldn't be here much longer. They all took a few sips of their beers and made small talk. Red's song came on, and she pulled Grady to his feet and dragged him over to the dance floor. At the same time, Kent got up to make his way to the back office. He was intent on getting the job done and hitting the road. Red wiggled her fingers at Kent as he walked past them.

Grady turned red in the face and stopped dancing. "What the fuck was that about?"

"What was what?" Red asked incredulously.

Grady wiggled his fingers, duplicating her wave to Kent. "That!" he growled. "Do you want him or me, because you can't have us both!"

Red lifted her chin defiantly. "I don't know what you're talking about.

I was just waving at him. Get over yourself."

"Well, quit flirting with him. You're with me. Don't be a tease!"

"Wh-what did you just call me?" Her eyes widened, and her nostrils flared with anger.

And just like that, all eyes were on them.

"You heard me. You do this every time we go out!" Grady took it up a notch and lightly shoved Red's shoulders. She stepped back a few paces.

"Don't you do that!" she shouted and put some power behind that exclamation by kicking her booted foot at Grady. He stepped out of the way just in time. He grabbed her around the waist and dropped her over his shoulder. "That's enough! You've caused enough of a scene already, little missy!" With that, he hauled her off the dance floor, despite her kicking and screaming.

Everyone moved out of the way as he made his way to the door. Kent came out of the back, pretending to dry his hands on his pants. He looked up and saw Red's panties bouncing in view beneath her short skirt. He shook his head and then caught the waitress's attention as he was about to walk past her. "I'm so sorry! These two do this all the time!"

"Oh, that's okay." She laughed nervously.

Kent winked at her, and she blushed. He made his exit. He was whistling as he made his way over to his partners in crime. They were aglow with the adventure—Red especially, as she jumped up and down with glee. "We did it again, boys!" They slid into the front seat to the sound of her giggles.

Kent went to open the driver's-side door. "Yes, we di—" But his words were halted by the piercing light that was suddenly cast upon them. "What the...?"

He turned and saw guns pointed at them. Someone yelled, "You're under arrest! Get your hands up!"

He was slammed against the car.

Grady and Red were being pulled from the car on the opposite side.

Kent was kicking himself. He knew they should have left this town sooner. He didn't utter a word as his homemade waist money bag was dropped onto the car hood.

Chapter 11

Saturday evening

Reyes couldn't have been prouder of his team. They'd executed the plan without anyone getting hurt. As it turned out, this band of thieves were unarmed. Brian Jackson thanked them for busting them outside his place. Reyes had called the other team off Chief's bar— the criminals had been apprehended. Chief was grateful they hadn't hit his place. A motel key had been found on them, allowing law enforcement to find the motel it belonged to. After securing a search warrant, Reyes found their pile of money neatly stashed in the bathroom vent.

The case was wrapped up, and the thieves were behind bars, pending their day in court. Reyes pulled up in front of Lucky's on Saturday night shortly before closing. Frank was busy behind the bar, which made Reyes happy. It allowed Reyes to slip back to the office without Frank seeing him.

Opening the middle desk drawer, he saw the bank deposit bag. He took the envelope of cash out of his waist band. Put the cash inside the bag, then closed the drawer. He tucked the empty envelope back in his jacket and walked out of the office, locking the door on his way out. It had not been locked when he'd entered. *Frank, you're still too trusting.*

With a smile on his face, he went up front and sat at the bar. He was going to celebrate. He smiled at Frank and ordered his drink. He knew Frank had already turned in the claim to his insurance company. This was just icing on the cake. He'd made sure that the portion he'd stuff inside the bank bag had not been included in the evidence count. Reyes was happy that he'd given in to the temptation to handle things this way. After all, Frank deserved a little more for his trouble.

~~~AFTER THE STORY~~~

What is After The Story (ATS)?

It's a wrap up after the story, my version of an Author's Note.

Do I need to read it?

No. No you do not need to read it.

What you May or May Not find in this section:

- Errors: Grammatical or spelling (the editor doesn't get to tidy this up). #notsorry

- Thoughts: About the book, and my fanciful ramblings.

- Inspiration, Gratitude, Life

- What's coming next

- Author Links, possible giveaways, and maybe a mystery

First, thank you for reading my story. I appreciate feedback and as an Indie author we are grateful when a review is left. Thank you to those who take the time to do that! <3

Second, I got the idea for this story after an opportunity presented itself to enter a short story anthology. IF you missed that, the title is still up for sale on Amazon in Paperback.

Make Them Pay – A Thriller Anthology

I had the title "Temptress" for quite a while. I have titles and stories pop into my head all the time. I only had the title for this, no story at the time until the anthology came into view. I knew I should us this title. As soon as I chose it, Grady, Kent and Red showed up, and they were quite the bunch! I loved writing their story. Sadly, for them, they were caught, but, they did steal money that didn't belong to them. Stealing IS wrong, they were not allowed to get away with it. LOL

While writing their story I realized I wanted to make this into a series. So, the Temptress Series was born. I am looking forward to getting back to them. I just have one novel to finish.

The Applicant – A psychological thriller coming later in 2021.

Be careful what you wish for.

Here is the link to sign up for my newsletter. I have TWO options for you. I value my readers time, so if you only want to know when the new book releases, there is that option. The 2nd option is the one for everything else (including the new release). In all honesty, you won't see many emails from me. I'd rather be writing/working on stories than putting together email content.

https://www.fallonraynes.com/contact-me

Third, I was thankful to have been a part of the anthology. It was a great opportunity that I am still shocked and excited to have been a part of. I met some really cool authors and enjoyed reading their stories. I've picked up a few new authors to read from it. To the gang, you ROCK! Keep WRITING!! <3

Thank you all for taking the time to read this story. IF you would like to follow me you can do that from any of the links at this link:

https://www.fallonraynes.com/follow-me

And, if you loved this story, please drop a review. I love reading them.
Have a blessed week. <3

Blessings,
Fallon
07/24/21

ABOUT THE AUTHOR

Fallon Raynes is a paper pusher by day, writer by night. Writing has been in Fallon's blood for as long as she can remember. Short stories and poems kept her mind at ease earlier on. Life's adventures have swirled in her mind to create some exaggerated stories that she's excited to put to paper and share with the world. To relax, Fallon enjoys watching the ID, Lifetime, and Hallmark channels, reading, and the outdoors.

Fallon resides in lower Michigan with her husband and fur-baby.
https://www.fallonraynes.com/books

Before you go, would you like to read a few chapters of my first novel Dangerous Ledges? Detectives Hannah and Reyes fist debuted in there.

Blurb:

Liza McAllister is newly divorced when she's talked into going on a cruise with her friend Chrissie. Determined to put her crazy ex behind her, Liza throws caution into the wind and indulges on some new clothes and a spacious cabin on the cruise ship. But someone else has other plans.

Ledge McAllister is hell-bent on reclaiming what is rightfully his. His life was turned upside down the day his wife walked out of his home. He will not lose her again. She belongs to him.

Warning: This psychological thriller holds no promise for a romantic ending. May cause chills.

Chapter 1

Saturday – Late October

His long legs reached the door first, slamming the heavy barrier in her face. He locked it from the other side. He would not lose this time. One way or another, she'd come around to his way of thinking.

She banged her fists against the wooden door and shouted, "Ledge, you crazy bastard! Let me out! Why are you doing this?"

Ledge laughed. "You're mine, Lizabeth! You don't get to leave me like you did!" *Never again will you leave me. I'll never let you go.*

She would not escape easily. There were no windows, and the lathe-and-plaster walls were not easy to punch a fist through. *I love old houses*, he thought. No one was around to hear her screams and commotion out in these middle-of-nowhere Michigan woods. *Besides, she won't continue much longer—she might break a nail.*

He walked down the hall to the kitchen, his stomach growling. "Time for something to eat."

As he grilled a PB&J, he noticed she had stopped beating on the door. He sighed in relief that she'd calmed down. He picked up his sandwich and took a bite, plotting his next move. He knew what he had to do, but he wasn't sure when he wanted to take action. Morning would shed light on that subject, pending his caged little tiger's mood. She had always been a little spitfire. He loved that about her. He'd misjudged the dose he'd used to knock her out and was thankful that he'd been able to place her petite body on the couch before she came to. "Your plan is in motion, Ledge, ol' boy."

***

She looked around the room. Anxiety attack over, she breathed heavily, concentrating on trying to regain a steady pattern. *No sense in crying. It won't do any good. You have to think.*

"Hard to do with a headache, Liza," she whispered to herself. What had he given her? Her recollection of how she had come to be in this room was fuzzy.

She had a bandage on her right hand, which was throbbing. Glass. She remembered broken glass on the floor. She closed her brown eyes, pulled the ponytail holder from her long brown hair, and clutched the sides of her head to massage her temples. After a few minutes, she opened her eyes and searched the small room.

There was a shabby old couch, a matching throw pillow, a blanket, and a bucket.

Wait! A bucket?

She walked over to it on unsteady legs. She'd seen those buckets before in a sporting-goods store. *Oh. My. God.* Shaking her head, she realized she might be trapped in this room for quite a while—because right next to the bucket was a roll of toilet paper. Bile rose in her throat as she shut down her anger. Being angry would not help her. She focused again on her breathing. *Think!*

Walking around the room, this time she noticed a cooler behind the couch, which she opened. There were bottles of water and a few apples. Sighing, she looked around again. Other than those few items, there was nothing else in the claustrophobic closet of a room—with no windows. Not a one. The carpeting was a horrendous burnt-orange color and well worn. She wondered how old the house was. At least the room had a light switch that worked, and she flicked it on and off a few times.

She figured the room had once had at least one window. Probably had been a small bedroom at one time. Tapping the walls, she could not find the studs. Everything sounded the same. *Darn it. Lathe-and-plaster walls. I will find that window.*

She walked to the thick wooden door and rested her back against it.

She listened closely but didn't hear anything. The place was like a vault.

Thinking back to her high-school drafting classes, she recalled the plans she used to draw. Visualizing what a typical house would look like, she walked forward to the opposite wall. *If this room was a bedroom at one time, and the door is behind me, this wall in front of me should have a window.*

She snapped her head around when she heard him humming outside the door. Rushing over to the couch, she sat down quickly while he unlocked the door. The smell of a grilled sandwich filled the room as he slid the tray along the floor with one of those reacher-handle things she'd seen on TV. She snickered, despite her worries. He was such an idiot. She wondered if she could have taken him by surprise, but didn't see a way. He had the upper hand for now.

"There you go, Lizabeth. Just like I used to make for you when we were married. Enjoy!"

"Bastard!" she hissed. It was all she could think to say.

"Ah, I've so missed your sweet-nothings." Pulling his long, handsome face into a smirk, he quickly ducked his towering frame out of view and locked the door again.

On cue, her stomach rumbled. She studied the tray of Lay's potato chips and the grilled PB&J. Despite her hunger, she couldn't bring herself to eat the food in front of her. He could have poisoned it, whatever. The simple fact that he'd made it was enough to make her gag.

Stomach growling again, she admitted that it was better to keep herself fueled. She doubted that he'd poisoned it—not so early in the game, anyway. *And what game was he playing?* She picked up the tray and sat down on the couch. Pulling apart the sandwich, she burned her finger on the dripping jelly. She cursed him and then more delicately probed the sandwich for anything suspicious. With a shrug of her shoulders—*to heck with it*—she put the sandwich back together and took a bite.

***

Turning from the door, he stalked back to the kitchen to clean up the mess from lunch. He couldn't trust her enough to ask her to do it. The thought made him irritable, so he pushed it out of his head. She really looked great since their divorce. Cheerleader curves back to where they were. Should have divorced her three years ago if he could have known she'd get her body back as a result. He shook his head. Again, his mind was taking him places he didn't want to go.

Time was on his side. Everyone thought she was in the Caribbean, relaxing and loving life. Yes, he had time. Smiling, he placed the clean dishes in the rack to dry. After wiping the counter, he quietly walked down the hall and heard small thudding noises. *Let her bang all she wants. She won't find a way out.*

Now whistling, he placed the dishrag on the sink to dry and headed to the back porch to watch the sunset. One of the relaxation techniques he'd learned from the doctor, who'd said, "Find something to focus on that brings you peace."

Have to stay focused and keep the demons at bay. So many colors across the sky tonight. She would love this sunset. Lizabeth had enjoyed the back-porch swing his dad had put in for his mom at their home. It had always relaxed Ledge, to hold Lizabeth's small frame in his strong arms as he gently rocked that swing. *I need to put a swing out here, too, if my plan works.* Whistling to himself, he picked up his stress ball and squeezed, squeezed, squeezed as a sense of calm washed over him.

Chapter 2

Knock, knock, tap, tap, knock. Nothing. Not ready to give up, she listened again for any sound outside of the door, then she started over on the wall across from the door. She had traversed the room and found an old nail lying on the floor. She used that as her marker. Her hand was getting sore from pounding the nail into the various places on the walls. She had marked the last row she tried and decided to go up from there about five inches. Thankfully, he wouldn't notice the marks easily, with the walls being in such a state of disrepair. The wallpaper was peeling in quite a few spots, and the old pattern of flowers covered the nail holes well.

She took a moment to rest and caught herself chewing on her freshly painted fingernails—done up in a Caribbean nail pattern especially for the trip. She sighed. Money down the drain.

It had started out in her savings account to go toward a surprise "honeymoon" for her and Ledge's anniversary this year. She had worked her tail off on a major project for almost two years and received a big bonus for her efforts. She had wanted to make it up to him for all her overtime. Frowning, her eyes focused on the wall as her mind replayed memories of the day that changed her plans, her life...

***

Caught in the Act

Early May

He sputtered, "Holy fuck! What are you— It's... it's not what it looks like."

"Oh, really? What do you expect me to think when I see my husband with his pants down around his ankles and a naked blonde bent over his desk?"

"Liza, I—" Ledge didn't finish the sentence as he struggled to pull up his drawers.

"Shut up! Save your lies! You've been lying to me for so many years... they're wasted on me." She saw the realization in his eyes; she had already suspected he was cheating again. "Yes, I know all about the marriedmen.com site and saw the profile you made."

Meanwhile, the blonde was trying to move as quickly as possible to gather her clothes and make an exit.

"Umm…" Liza held up her hand, eyebrow raised, and blocked the doorway. "Sorry, Blondie. I have something to say to you. I don't care if he's paying you or if you think fucking a married man is fun, but karma is a bitch. When you catch the man you love with another woman under him, remember today, and you'll know exactly how I feel at this very minute."

Vibrating with anger and hurt, she heard Ledge start to speak and whipped around to cut him off. "You cheating bastard! You don't get to do this to me anymore."

She walked out of his office on shaky legs with as much grace as she could muster, leaving the dumbfounded cheats behind. Reaching her truck, she slid into the seat, slammed the door, and finally let the tears fall. *This will be the last time he hurts me.* No amount of information from the PI could have prepared her for the scene she'd just witnessed. With a deep breath, she wiped her tears and headed home. The last thing she wanted was for him to see her crying.

***

After quickly packing the rest of her belongings that she hadn't had time to pack before she'd caught him in the act, she pressed the reset-to-factory-settings button on her phone. While she watched it erase everything left on the phone that she hadn't already removed, she murmured to herself, "I wish I could do that with all my memories of him." Liza pulled the house key off her key ring and placed it on the counter next to the cell phone and her wedding ring. "I won't need those anymore."

She brushed her hands together, satisfied. There would be no way for him to hound her while she tried to re-bundle the pieces of her life. Divorce wasn't desirable, but sometimes there was no other answer. Taking one last look around the house to ensure she had everything she wanted to take, she drew a deep breath and let it out slowly as she turned to leave for good. All the memories, all the projects, all that time... wasted. Packing had kept her focused. With that done, the tears threatened to spill again. Pulling a tissue from her pocket, she wiped them away.

Liza locked the front door on her way to her shiny white truck she had purchased in anticipation of this day. The day she had dreaded. She put the truck in gear, slowly pulled out of the drive with the trailer shadowing her, and didn't look back. Referencing her mental to-do list, she checked off a few things:

- Catch Cheating Bastard - Check
- Leave Cheating Bastard - Check
- Get moved into a new place - On my way now
- Call a good divorce attorney - Dialing now
- RESET LIFE – Working on it.

***

A Week Later at Liza's Office

"Hello, I have a delivery for a Lizabeth McAllister."

"That's me."

Smiling, the deliveryman handed her the flowers. "Have a nice day," he said and tipped his nonexistent hat. Before she even read the card, Liza's hackles were up. She glanced at Ann, their receptionist, who had quirked her eye up in question. Liza ignored it and excused herself. She made it back to her office and set the flowers on her desk as she looked at the card— from guess who?

I'm very sorry. I miss you. Please call me.

She tossed the card on her desk, pushed the flowers to the farthest corner, reining in her need to smash them against the wall. Trying to brush off her anger, Liza called her best friend, Trinity Gold. "I need to talk."

They wasted no time in making plans to meet at Trinity's house that evening.

***

Trinity's mouth dropped open, her expression one of shock. "He really signed it that way? 'Love, Cheating Bastard'?"

They were sitting in the Golds' living room, each in a comfortable chair, wrapped in a blanket, with a hot drink nearby—tea for Trinity and cocoa for Liza.

"No. I added that part."

Trinity put a hand to her heart. "Oh, goodness. You had me there. But he might as well have written it." She sniffed and took a sip of her tea.

The drama queen. Liza's best friend. And Liza loved every bit of her. Especially during times like these.

"Yeah, that's my automatic response whenever I think of him." With her face coiled in disgust, Liza reached for her hot cocoa on the coffee table, being careful not to spill it on herself or Trinity's furniture. "When does Oliver get home? Am I imposing?"

"Not for another hour or so. He's helping a friend move a new refrigerator into his man cave. And, thankfully, Abbie is spending the night at a friend's house tonight. The last time those twelve-year-old girls got together over here, it was after two in the morning before I finally stopped hearing the giggles coming from her bedroom."

Liza laughed, knowing full well how much Trinity loved her family and being a mother. Abbie was a sweet child and was definitely going to be a heartbreaker with her blond curls and eyes of the brightest blue. She was already attracting attention from the boys, Trinity had told her recently. Ollie was certainly going to have his hands full trying to keep the guys off their lawn.

Trinity adjusted the blanket that covered her lap and cleared her throat before saying, "Uh, are you sure you don't want to talk to him?"

"Hell to the NO! You must still be a sucker for his hot looks. Hmm?" Liza gave her friend a teasing smirk. "Believe me, he's not the same tall, dark, and handsome football player we used to cheer for, the guy I fell in love with. I have *zero* desire to be with a repetitive cheater and liar and general jerk. It's not easy walking around town, looking at every pretty young face, thinking he may have slept with her too. It makes me sick every time I think about it."

Trinity frowned. "I've noticed you've lost some weight since—" she flailed her hands "—you found out he was back to his cheating ways."

Liza shrugged. "A bit, I guess. I've had a lot on my mind, for obvious reasons. And now this, of course."

"I get it. I do." Trinity tilted her head as her expression softened. "So, what did you do with the flowers?"

"I took them to the nursing home and asked if anyone there was having a bad day and could use a bouquet. I made the old gal cry when I took them to her room, but at least those were tears of happiness."

"Best thing to do."

"Yeah, I was glad they did someone some good. I cringe now when I think back, because flowers were his go-to move when he was feeling bad about something he'd done. I don't want or need anything that reminds me of him. It'll be hard enough facing the twins when I go see them this week at college. I'll have to explain the divorce then."

"So, Ledge hasn't mentioned anything to them, huh? You would have heard something."

"He's probably hoping it will all go away. It's just as well; the twins are finishing up their spring finals. They stay at the dorms to keep the distractions to a minimum, so they won't notice I've left the house."

There was silence between them as Liza's mind whirled, and Trinity waited to jump in as needed. Liza had never felt more fortunate for their friendship than at that very moment. Trinity knew some of the sad stories of Liza's life with Ledge, but mostly, Liza had tried to keep things to herself… because she wanted to believe it wasn't so.

Now, though, she was ready to spill her guts. "Looking back on all those times I'd *thought* he was cheating … well, I was right all along. All that trying to 'better himself' bullshit, quitting smoking so he could 'live longer for me and the kids.' Ha! I went through hell while he was on that mind-altering drug, Cantril."

"Yeah, I remember you mentioning it every now and then."

"It totally messed him up as far as having control over his emotions. Zero to crazy in less than one second. He did quit smoking. I'll give him that. But he didn't quit *boinking*. I found out his online dating profile was started over two years ago! And then the naked blonde on his desk." Liza grabbed at her hair and yanked from frustration as she bent forward and put her elbows on her knees. "She had to know he was married. I mean, our pictures are right there in his office! How does a woman do something like that, knowing he's married?"

"I honestly don't understand that, either. The whole thing is so trashy." Trinity waved her hand in the air and wrinkled her nose, as if trying to push away a nasty smell. "So, you haven't actually spoken with him since, uh, you caught him with his pants down?"

"No, and quite frankly, I'm surprised he hasn't tried to show up at my office. I think he knows he won't be welcome there, and unless he's tried to follow me home, he doesn't know where I'm staying yet. So far, so good! I don't need to see him again until the day in court when the divorce will be final."

"How much longer?"

"About a month, the attorney said, unless Ledge contests what we've proposed. And he shouldn't protest, since I don't want anything from that house. I've taken what belongs to me, and that's all I want. The house was his parents' before their accident, and it never really felt like ours when I moved in. Anyway, my attorney isn't very happy because we have the proof to go for more, but I don't want it to drag on like the brutal divorce Chrissie went through. I want to be done with him." Chrissie was another cherished friend from their group.

"You think he's received the papers yet?"

"I haven't heard. They were supposed to call me after he was served. I told him I was done this time, so it shouldn't shock him too much."

"Well, I'm sure that will let him know how serious you are. I'm surprised he hasn't found you and tried to make up, like he did last year. He hid his craziness from Ollie and me very well, I have to say. I had no idea he had gone berserk and tried to hurt you. I'm sorry you had to go through all that, Liza. What a freaking nightmare."

"Nothing either of you could have done. It got scary a few times, but he regained his self-control before anything physical happened. The verbal part was hard enough to handle. The words still ring in my ears. I'd told him that the next time he went off on me, I was gone. I guess he figured if he didn't get angry, he could get away with cheating instead, and I would never find out. Hard not to think something's going on when he comes home from work and immediately takes a shower before heading to the den to watch TV." Liza set her drink down on the table and rewrapped herself in the blanket. She shuddered and said, "Darn, Trin. Just because its spring doesn't mean it's warm. Are you going to turn your heat back on?"

Laughing at her friend, Trinity grabbed the cups off the table and headed for the kitchen. "You don't pay our bills, woman. This has to last, and unless it drops below forty degrees outside, it stays off. Besides, I sleep better when it's cooler in the house." She stuck her tongue out at Liza as she walked to the kitchen.

Glancing around the living room, Liza noticed a photo of the two couples—she and Ledge, Trinity and Oliver—taken during the New Year's party they'd attended this year.

She sighed, a little bit of jealousy creeping in. Trin and Ollie had been inseparable in high school and still were. The "Ledge and Liza" in that picture used to be the same way. Staring at the New Year's photo, Liza looked at it for the first time with a clearer vision. It was a farce. Ledge had already been cheating long before that night. Liza's backtracking had led her to that conclusion, which pushed her to hire a private investigator to ferret out the truth. Liza turned away from that memory.

Tears threatened again, and she wiped them away before Trin entered the living room with a heaping bowl of Liza's favorite ice cream: Chocolate Overload. Trin sure knew how to make her feel better. Smiling, Liza accepted the bowl and dug in before Trin had a chance to sit down. With her short legs curled beneath her and the blanket in place, Trinity asked the hard question, something Liza suspected her friend had wanted to know for a long time. "I know it's none of my business, and you can tell me to fuck off, but how many times has he cheated on you?"

Liza set her bowl down on the coffee table as the slow burn started at the pit of her stomach. No longer interested in her favorite indulgence, she formed her words before speaking. Humiliation washed across her face as Trin watched her.

"It was about a year and a half after we were married. One night, after we had a great night out dancing and laughing like we hadn't in a few months, he told me. Ledge blurted it out in such a rush that I hadn't time to absorb the words. He must have felt guilty. Said he would never do it again if I'd forgive him. It was with someone he worked with. He said it was because she came on to him, and he couldn't understand why and wanted to find out." Liza sighed, gathered her composure, and continued.

"When I told him I was not going to stop him from seeing her, he didn't know what to say. I knew if he wasn't going to be faithful then… well, I wasn't going to have a marriage with him. I told him so in no uncertain terms. It was like it flipped a switch in him, Trin. He stopped seeing her, started courting me again, and then the woman ended up moving away shortly after. I guess she couldn't take the embarrassment at work. Things were very good between us after that. I still kept an eye on things, though, because I figured, for sure, he would do it again, but he never strayed—at least not until sometime in the past few years. Of course, what do I really know? He could have strayed… I don't know, a hundred times."

Unchecked tears ran down Liza's face as she spoke, and Trinity's eyes were brimming as well. Trinity left the chair and wrapped her arms around her best friend. "Just let it out."

And Liza bawled like a baby.

You can look here to find Dangerous Ledges:

Amazon US: https://amzn.to/37dAjCC
Amazon CA: https://amzn.to/2SkliLe
Amazon UK: https://amzn.to/2Smptq0
Amazon AU: https://amzn.to/2Soxvi6
Nook: https://bit.ly/37LUFa9
iTunes: https://apple.co/2SoRtsT
Kobo: http://bit.ly/2Spm49U
https://www.fallonraynes.com/follow-me